Love Puppies

WE'RE HERE TO HELP!

Best Friends Furever

JaNay Brown-Wood

SCHOLASTIC INC.

Copyright © 2023 by JaNay Brown-Wood

Interior illustrations by Eric Proctor, © 2023 Scholastic Inc.

All rights reserved. Published by Scholastic Inc., *Publishers since 1920*. SCHOLASTIC and associated logos are trademarks and/or registered trademarks of Scholastic Inc.

The publisher does not have any control over and does not assume any responsibility for author or third-party websites or their content.

No part of this publication may be reproduced, stored in a retrieval system, or transmitted in any form or by any means, electronic, mechanical, photocopying, recording, or otherwise, without written permission of the publisher. For information regarding permission, write to Scholastic Inc., Attention: Permissions Department, 557 Broadway, New York, NY 10012.

This book is a work of fiction. Names, characters, places, and incidents are either the product of the author's imagination or are used fictitiously, and any resemblance to actual persons, living or dead, business establishments, events, or locales is entirely coincidental.

ISBN 978-1-338-83408-6

10 9 8 7 6 5 4 3 2   23 24 25 26 27

Printed in the U.S.A.   40

First printing 2023

Book design by Omou Barry

Decorative design border art © Shutterstock.com

To my one and only Lonie and her
Love Puppies, Lacy and Penny

Fall in love with each paw-fectly sweet adventure!

TABLE OF CONTENTS

Chapter 1
Early Morning Message

Buzz, buzz! Buzz, buzz!

Rosie's doggie ears perked up at the sound that buzzed from down the hall of the Love Puppy Doghouse. She knew exactly what it was: the Crystal Bone. Her excellent ears could hear it vibrate. She could also see that it was flashing like crazy. Its blinking alert lit up the dim morning, even though it was all the way in the living room.

"Uh-oh," she said to herself. "The sun is not even up yet. Must be important." Rosie hopped out of her comfy doggie bed and bounded across the floor. Sleep would have to wait.

But just as she reached the door, something stopped her. A tickle or an itch—right in her chest, where her heart beat. She sat on her hind legs and looked down. A faint light seemed to shine ever so slightly beneath her fur. It shimmered for just a moment. Then it was gone.

That was strange, Rosie thought, gently touching

her chest with the front of her paw. Then the *buzz*, *buzz* of the Crystal Bone reminded Rosie she had a job to do. She shook the strange glow from her mind and raced into the hallway.

"Rise and shine, Love Puppies," she called. Not one of the other pups stirred.

Rosie tried again. "Upsy-daisy," she said, a little louder this time, "we've got an urgent message waiting!"

"All right, all right," said Barkley the dachshund, stretching his short legs. "I'm up."

"Great," said Rosie as she wagged her tail. Barkley and the rest of the puppies dragged themselves out of their rooms and down the hallway.

"This couldn't wait?" Noodles, the labradoodle, asked as she slouched past Rosie. "I was having the best dream ever. It was a beautiful day and there were rainbows and sunrays crisscrossing the sky!" Noodles wore a long nightcap that hung from her ears. It had a fuzzy ball on the very end.

"You know, even magical pups like us need our beauty sleep," whined Clyde, the shar-pei puppy, as he flew sleepily through the air. He yawned so widely that he almost bumped into the wall before landing on the rug in the main living room.

"I know, I know. But when the Crystal Bone calls, that means we've got work to do!" Rosie hurried into the living room after the other pups.

Each wall in the living room had large windows covered by paw-printed curtains. Small pots of beautiful flowers decorated each windowsill. Rosie had grown them herself. As she padded past them, the flowers opened and leaned toward her as if they were waving hello.

This was the Love Puppy den: an enchanted place perfect for four magical pups to eat, sleep, play, and make plans to help kids in need! Along the walls hung four giant banners, each with a moving picture of one of the Love Puppies showing off their special magic—and in their signature colors.

Rosie and her soft golden fur stood out on the bright pink banner. She was a golden retriever with flower magic, the power to grow plants and flowers whenever she wanted.

A blue banner showed Clyde, a wrinkly sharpei with the ability to fly. He didn't even need a cape!

The orange banner showcased Noodles, a shaggy labradoodle with the power to control weather and its different elements.

And the purple banner displayed Barkley, a tiny dachshund who could transform into anything he pleased!

These Love Puppies had hearts of gold, and helping human kids was their favorite thing to do. Even if it meant waking up earlier than usual.

The banner-pups jumped up at the sight of the real Love Puppies entering the room. They wiggled and danced across the walls. Noodles waved to her look-alike, and blew a gentle wind, causing each of the banners to flutter in her breeze. All the banner-pups yipped with excitement.

Clyde let out another gigantic yawn.

"Still sleepy?" asked Barkley. "I can help!" The heart-shaped pads on his paws glowed bright purple. Instantly, his long body morphed into a bright purple pillow.

"Paw-fect!" yipped Noodles. She and Clyde snuggled next to their Pillow-Barkley with a sigh.

7

"Okay, we've got serious business," Rosie began. "A new mission!" The look in Rosie's brown eyes told them this would be an important one.

"In that case, we're all ears!" said Clyde.

Rosie hurried to the center of the room where the oversized Crystal Bone blinked pink, blue, orange, and purple. The giant bone flashed, buzzed, and floated in the air whenever there was an urgent message.

While flower magic was Rosie's thing, she also was the only pup who could receive messages from the Crystal Bone. It served as a magical window into the human world during times of need.

And with how brightly the magical beacon was blinking right now was certainly a time of need for someone, somewhere!

When Rosie reached the Crystal Bone, she stood on her hind legs, placed both paws on it, and closed her eyes. The heart-shaped pads on Rosie's paws glowed a brilliant pink and soon a glittering *whoosh* of wind filled the room. The glitter swirled around her and the pups, ruffling the banners and the picture-pups, too. They howled from their hanging fabric.

Then, as suddenly as it had begun, the wind stopped and all was quiet.

Rosie opened her eyes. "Oh dear," she said.

The other pups ran over to where she stood, including Barkley, who had transformed back into his pup body.

Rosie pulled her paws from the Crystal Bone, pads up, as if she was holding something special. A puff of glitter floated above her upturned paws, slowly transforming into a small pink hologram of a human girl. The pups watched as tears fell from the girl's eyes. She ran over to her mother, held her tightly, and cried some more.

"Oh no!" whined Barkley. His wet nose was so close to the hologram in Rosie's paws that he could almost touch it. "She looks so sad!"

A tiny rain cloud drizzled over Noodles's head.

The flowers lining the windows drooped a little bit. Clyde sniffed loudly.

The three pups huddled around Rosie and the tiny pink human. They whimpered and howled and slowly wagged their tails.

"Love Puppies," Rosie said, raising the hologram into the air. "This is Meiko, and she needs our help!"

Chapter 2
Mission Meiko

As the pups gathered around, Rosie placed her paws back on the Crystal Bone. That way, a larger picture of Meiko would project from the Bone right onto the ceiling. Each pup looked up as her profile appeared.

MEIKO ITO
Age: 8
Grade: Third
School: Cloverfield Elementary
Problem: No friends at her brand-new school

The Crystal Bone then showed the Love Puppies scenes from Meiko's life before she changed schools, like a movie playing across the ceiling. They saw her smiling and laughing, dancing and singing, and playing with so many different friends. One clip showed Meiko roller-skating. Another showed her baking—and devouring—a piece of cake. Then, the Bone zoomed in on a scene of Meiko picking up a tiny puppy and sweetly kissing its furry head.

Noodles pawed at the ceiling as if she was petting the images of Meiko. "I like her already!"

As Rosie sat down on the carpet, the projected images disappeared.

"Today is Meiko's third day at school," Rosie said. "She hasn't made any friends yet."

"Nobody to wrestle with?" said Barkley, jumping playfully onto Clyde. The two rolled and yipped before landing on their bellies. *Wump!* "Even after three days?"

"No one to tickle," Rosie said, ruffling Noodles's fur. "Or to smell the roses with! Our job is an important one," she continued. "We must find a friend for Meiko—and fast!"

"But who?" asked Clyde.

"Good question," said Rosie. "We need to go on a friend hunt!"

"How will we do that?" asked Clyde. He was always full of questions.

"We'll search the school for the perfect match," said Rosie.

"What will we do after that?" Clyde wondered aloud. His ears wiggled wildly as more questions fluttered in his head. "And what if we can't find a friend? What if she goes a whole *week* without one?" Clyde asked. His shar-pei eyes grew wider with each question.

"Whoa, Clydie," said Rosie calmly. She placed

a paw on his back. "Deep breaths, pup. Deep breaths."

Clyde inhaled deeply and filled up his small chest. Then he let it out slowly.

"See. That's better. No need to worry," said Rosie, "we'll take things one paw at a time."

"Got it," said Clyde. "One paw at a time."

"I think we should start with the third-grade classes," said Noodles with a confident yip. "That way Meiko and her new best bud will have plenty in common."

"Me too," added Barkley.

"Sounds good to me!" Rosie said.

"I am glad we are going to help," said Noodles. "I

can tell Meiko has a kind heart. We'll need to find someone who is sweet and nice."

"But who also likes having fun!" added Barkley, turning himself into a ball and bouncing across the floor. Clyde chased the purple ball excitedly. He never missed a chance to play fetch.

"And someone who loves . . ." Rosie began, but the rest chimed in at the same time to say, "PUPPIES!" Each of their tails wagged like dancing caterpillars.

Rosie's chest tickled again, but she pretended not to notice. Instead, she said, "Can we do it, Love Puppies?" placing her paw out in front of her. The heart-shaped pad glowed a beautiful pink again, just as it did every time her magic was activated. But this time, her magic would do more than just grow flowers or listen to the Crystal Bone. This time— with the help of the other pups—her magic would save the day!

The other puppies joined in, placing their paws on top of Rosie's. Each of their heart-shaped pads glowed, too: blue for Clyde, orange for Noodles, and purple for Barkley.

"With the power of love—anything is paw-sible!" shouted Rosie. "Love Puppies, go!"

Whoosh!

Rosie's magic words and the pups' activated power opened the Doggie Door—a heart-shaped portal that swirled with magic and adventure. On one side was the Love Puppy Doghouse, their home. But on the other side? Well, that could be ANYWHERE! All Rosie had to do was picture the place in her head and, *whoosh*, it appeared.

And right now, the place she imagined was a hidden spot behind the third-grade building of Cloverfield Elementary School.

Each pup jumped through the spinning portal and landed with a thump in a cluster of bushes.

"First, we'll check Mr. Barnett's class in Room 13," Rosie told them. "Then, we'll head to Mrs. Nicholson's class in Room 12. Let's get to work, Pups. And no matter what, *don't* get spotted . . ."

. . . or else.

Chapter 3
The Right Class

Not getting spotted was an important rule. Just one glimpse of the Love Puppies by an unsuspecting human and all attention would be on the team of puppies.

Who could blame the poor humans? The pups

were adorable! Big, floppy ears. Soft, fuzzy fur. Giant puppy dog eyes. No human could resist them! Being spotted meant they would be picked up, played with, and cuddled all day long. If that happened, Meiko would never find a friend.

So of course, staying hidden was a must!

"Now, how do you suppose we get into that classroom?" asked Noodles.

"The door could work," said Clyde with a wink.

"True," said Barkley, "but we'd probably be spotted." He and Clyde scratched their heads and climbed out of the poky bushes.

"Look! There!" said Rosie, pointing her paw at the building. "The window. Noodles, give us cover while we fly up and look inside. I'm sure we'll be able to find the perfect friend for Meiko through the window."

"Good plan!" said Clyde.

Rosie jumped onto Clyde's back as his paw pads began to glow a vibrant blue and Noodles's shined orange. Right above Noodles's head, a fog cloud appeared. The cloud grew bigger and bigger until it was the perfect size for hiding Clyde and Rosie. Up they went.

"What do you see?" Barkley said in a loud whisper.

Clyde peered through Noodles's cloud and into the window. Inside, the children sat in pairs working on math problems with paper, pencils, and . . .

"COOKIES," said Clyde. "I see cookies!" His tummy rumbled and reminded him that with all the hubbub of the early morning, he'd missed breakfast.

"And lots of kids," Rosie added.

"See Meiko anywhere?" asked Noodles.

"I see . . . kids . . ." whispered Clyde, ". . . kids . . . kids . . . cookies . . ."

"Focus on the not-cookies stuff, please," reminded Barkley.

"Let's head back down," Rosie said through a giggle. "I think we've seen enough."

But once Rosie's and Clyde's paws were back on solid ground, her good mood drooped. "There was no sign of Meiko."

"And we didn't see a perfect new friend for her either," said Clyde. "Everybody already seems matched up in this class."

"Aww, poodle-sticks!" said Noodles.

The thought of Meiko spending another day without a pal sent the pups into soft whimpers of sorrow.

"Don't lose hope yet! We still have to check Room 12," reminded Rosie. "You two stay here. Barkley, come with me. We'll be back soon!" Clyde and Noodles crouched in their hiding place as Rosie and Barkley raced toward the next schoolroom.

"There it is," Rosie said, "Mrs. Nicholson's class."

Rosie and Barkley hurried onto the lawn right in front of Room 12. Rosie closed her eyes and stooped down. Her paws began to glow. All around her, little blades of grass pushed up from the ground. Then, Rosie's magic made her a curtain of daisies—a bunch of pretty flowers springing from the lawn around Rosie's body—just high enough to hide her, but not so high that any humans passing by might wonder about it.

"Ready?" she whispered, poking her nose out from the flower curtain.

"Ready," said Barkley. All at once, Barkley's little dachshund legs got skinnier and longer as his tummy and back spread out like a Frisbee and he shrank to the size of a bug. And his ears morphed into tiny antennae sitting on top of a beetle-shaped head.

"You're so tiny!" said Rosie.

"Perfect for squeezing under doors," said Beetle-Barkley's bug-sized voice before he scurried off into Room 12.

But all he found was a dark, empty room. It did smell nice, though. Like a big bowl of lemons.

Is this the right class? he wondered, scrambling across the hard floor and up a wall for a better look. *Is anybody here?*

Nope. Not one human in sight. Where were they?

Beetle-Barkley squeezed back under the door.

Once outside, his buggy legs scurried across the sidewalk and over to Rosie.

"I thought Room 12 was Mrs. Nicholson's room," squeaked Barkley. "But no one was there."

"That *is* Mrs. Nicholson's classroom," said Rosie. She was sure the Crystal Bone had told her so. She could see the number 12 on the wall. "Hmm. The class must have gone someplace else." Rosie paused and lifted her nose in the air. "What's that scent?" she asked, sniffing around. "Smells like . . ." She lowered her nose to Barkley and took another good whiff. "LEMONS! You smell lemony-fresh," she giggled, sniffing him again.

Beetle-Barkley transformed himself back into

Puppy-Barkley as Rosie sniffed him playfully.

"I guess the classroom rubbed off on me," he said. "It smelled just like lemons in there."

"Paw-fect," Rosie said. "Since you smell like the classroom does, I bet the kids do, too. We should be able to find them now!" Rosie sniffed at the air again. Her nose tingled. She picked up the soft scent of lemons. "This way!" she called excitedly.

Rosie and Barkley kept to the shadows, following their noses.

"There they are!" barked Barkley.

Meiko and her classmates were in the school's garden. But it was all the way on the other side of the school, way out past the schoolyard.

"Woof, that's a long way to go without being spotted," said Barkley with worry in his voice.

How would they get all the way to the garden without somebody seeing them?

Chapter 4
Garden Mess

The school sat on a big block with most of the classroom buildings in one corner. The blacktop, playground, and grassy schoolyard stretched across the middle of the block. And in the farthest corner was the school's garden. Large ceramic pots with flower bushes lined each side of the garden fence.

It was definitely a long way for two pint-sized puppies.

"We've got this," said Rosie. "But how will we hide along the way?"

"I know!" said Barkley. "I've got just the trick!"

Barkley's paws began to glow. His tiny belly stretched and flattened into a long blanket, but his head, feet, and tail didn't change. From his blanket-belly, little green hairs that looked like grass began to grow, and in one blink, Barkley turned green.

"You look like a seasick flying squirrel!" said Rosie with a chuckle.

"What can I say?" Barkley winked teasingly as

31

he draped himself over Rosie. "I'm one fly guy!"

"Good one, silly pup!" laughed Rosie. "Let's go!"

The two of them stepped out of the shadows and onto the grassy lawn. This was perfect because nature and the grass were Rosie's territory. She slinked down, making the blades of grass along their path grow taller. This helped to cover her and Blanket-Barkley even more. Quickly, the two hidden pups hurried across the schoolyard and toward the garden for a closer look.

"There she is!" whispered Barkley. They had only ever seen Meiko as a hologram. Seeing her in person felt like finding a long-lost friend.

Rosie's heart tingled again. Was the strange glow

back? But just as she began to look, she tripped on her feet and went tumbling head over paws. She landed on her belly. *OOMPH!*

"Are you all right?" asked Barkley as he jumped on top of her to keep her covered.

"Sorry, I got distracted. We're almost there." She and Barkley sped across the last stretch of the field.

Inside, the garden was beautiful. It had a wood chip path that circled the eight raised flower beds. Each one was painted a different color, with child-sized handprints decorating every side. Two hoses that led to a water spigot outside the garden's gate lay coiled like giant snakes.

And oh, the colors! Yellow sunflowers and orange

lilies bloomed everywhere. There were bright red peppers, purple eggplants, and every shade of green in the leaves of the plants. Rosie sighed in delight, her nose kissed by the pretty scent of happy flowers. Even though she was tempted to use magic to make them dance, staying hidden was more important.

The little garden was busy with movement and sound, too. Three clucking chickens strutted around the space, pecking at dried corn that some of the children had scattered for them. Other kids watered the vegetables and flowers growing in the garden beds. The teacher called out directions as the children worked, snipping leaves, patting soil, and tending to plants.

But Meiko sat alone on an upside-down bucket. Her arms wrapped herself in a hug, and her eyes were sad as she stared at the ground.

Rosie wished she could hug Meiko. She was sure she'd be able to make the girl smile instead of frown.

Giggles filled the air as a group of girls near Meiko kneeled next to a healthy, green daisy plant with a tiny flower bud springing from the stem. The girls chatted while sprinkling the plant with a watering can.

"That one needs a drink, too, Eliza!" called one of the girls, pointing to a flagging sprout in the bed closest to Meiko. Eliza walked over and poured water on it. But she didn't say anything to Meiko. She didn't even glance Meiko's way.

"Wow, look!" Eliza exclaimed. The stem of the just-watered plant began growing taller and taller, inch by inch, right before their eyes. Its leaves spread out just a bit, and its buds changed from green to pink in one flick of a tail. "That's amazing! Watering really *does* help!"

But instead of talking to Meiko about what they'd just seen, Eliza hurried back to her friends. "Did you see what just happened?" she gushed to them as they moved on to a different flower bed.

"Puppy toes! I thought for sure that would have sparked a conversation between Meiko and that girl." Rosie watched Meiko stare at the plant suspiciously, slowly moving away from it.

"It was worth a try," said Barkley. Rosie nodded in agreement.

The two pups looked around. Nobody seemed interested in sitting next to Meiko. Instead, her classmates all worked together, planting seeds and caring for the plants.

But really, Rosie wasn't surprised. She knew that moving to a new school near the end of the year had to be tough, especially if you were shy. And Meiko definitely seemed shy.

Plus, everybody already had friends by now. Adding new ones was sometimes a very hard thing to do.

Rosie held her breath to keep from whimpering.

She and Barkley were too close. Their soft sounds would absolutely be heard by the kids. But seeing Meiko so sad made Rosie want to rush over and give her puppy kisses all over her face.

"Oh my! There you are," said a nearby voice.

Uh-oh! Had they been spotted?

"I was looking for you, Meiko," said the voice.

"I'm here, Mrs. Nicholson," said Meiko.

"Good. I was wondering if you'd help me with the sunflowers. I could use another pair of hands."

"Okay." Meiko stood.

"Girls," Mrs. Nicholson said to Eliza and the group of friends Rosie had noticed earlier, "maybe a few of you can help me, too."

"Of course, Mrs. Nicholson."

"Look!" said Rosie. She and Barkley wagged their tails with excitement as the girls followed the teacher. They were smiling at Meiko! Eliza even handed Meiko the watering can. Could it be?

"Maybe *they* can be her friends," yipped Rosie. "Not just one of them, but *all* of them!"

"Yes, maybe!" said Barkley happily. "They are all going to work together, just like friends do!"

"I think we've done it!" said Rosie. "We've got to get back to Noodles and Clyde and let them know!"

With the same cover that they used before, Barkley and Rosie ran across the field and back to the bushes behind Room 13.

Just as they reached the bush that hid Clyde and Noodles, the recess bell rang.

"Pups! Pups! We did it! We found..." Rosie stopped cold in her puppy tracks. "What's wrong?" she asked Clyde and Noodles as they huddled together beneath the bush, whining loudly.

"We checked a few of the other classrooms, too, just to be sure!" cried Clyde.

"No luck at all! We'll never find a friend for Meiko!" sobbed Noodles.

"Dry your tears, Pups!" said Rosie. "We've got great news for you!"

"She's already found some new friends!" added Barkley.

Clyde's ears perked up. "Yip yip hooray!" he barked with a quick flying-flip of joy.

"Since it's recess time now, we'll show you!" said Rosie. "Noodles, give us some cover, please."

Noodles puffed up another cloud as Barkley transformed into a magic carpet for Rosie and Noodles to ride. With their disguises, and Clyde leading the way, they jetted off toward the playground.

"See right there . . . Wait, where's Meiko?" asked Barkley.

The pups found the group of girls from before, laughing and playing hopscotch. But Meiko was nowhere to be found. She wasn't with them.

"There she is!" said Noodles.

Meiko sat all alone next to the sandbox, picking some wildflowers that grew beside it. She gently plucked each flower, then tied the stems together to make a bracelet. A few lonely tears fell down her cheeks. As the pups got closer, they could hear her whispering, "I miss my friends. I miss my old home. I hate it here!"

So much for the success of Mission Meiko.

"Pups," said Rosie, "this is going to be harder than we thought. We should head back to the bushes and come up with another plan."

Just as Magic Carpet–Barkley started to turn the carpet around, he stopped midair. "Flying Frisbees! Looky there!"

The pups all glanced in the direction of a swing set. On one of the swings sat a girl, all by herself. She didn't smile or laugh or even swing. Instead, she kicked at the dirt under her shoes.

"Who do you think that is?" asked Clyde.

The girl stood up from the swing set and headed back toward the classrooms. As she passed by Room 12, she stopped, kneeled down, and picked a few daisies that grew in a bundle on the lawn.

"Oopsie-daisy," said Rosie. "I guess I forgot to reverse my magic."

The girl cradled the daisies in her hand. Then, she sat down against the wall of Room 15 and pulled out a small bag filled with flowers. She gently added the daisies, closed the bag, and put it back into her pocket. She didn't move again until the bell rang and her class lined up in front of the door.

Once recess was over and all the kids were back inside their classrooms, the pups watched through the window as this new girl sat at a desk labeled "Jasmine." She pulled the bag back out and added the new flowers to a small jar on her desk. The jar already had some flowers in it, and a little water at the bottom.

"There," said the girl, smiling at her miniature bouquet. "Maddie would have loved these," she whispered to herself.

"Emergency meeting!" cried Rosie. "We're going to need the Crystal Bone!"

Once they were back behind the bushes, the pups placed their paws in the center of their circle. Then Rosie barked the magic words.

"With the power of love—anything is paw-sible! Crystal Bone, we need you."

Chapter 5
Jasmine Who?

There, hidden behind the bushes, the Doggie Door floated in the air. But the pups didn't jump through it. They were seeking the help of the Crystal Bone—in the human world.

"This only works if no humans can see us,"

reminded Rosie. She lifted her glowing paws and turned them, causing the portal to lie flat on the grass, and magically the Crystal Bone appeared— half of it still in the Doghouse, half of it poking into the real world.

"Magic is pup-tastic!" Clyde said with a joyful air twirl.

"Okay," said Rosie, "we need some information on another human child. Her name is Jasmine and she also goes to Cloverfield Elementary." Rosie stood on her hind legs and placed her paws on the Crystal Bone.

A picture of a small girl with freckles appeared on the Bone with the name "Jasmine Ortega" beside it.

"Nope, that's not her," said Noodles.

The Crystal Bone showed another completely new girl. None of the pups recognized her either.

"How many Jasmines are there at Cloverfield?" asked Clyde.

"Ten, according to the Crystal Bone," said Rosie.

"That's going to take too long!" said Barkley. "How about we give the Bone some clues? Our Jasmine had pretty, dark skin."

"With brown eyes and really curly black hair," added Clyde.

"Oh, and she went into Room 15," said Noodles.

Suddenly, a new picture glowed from the Crystal Bone's glassy surface.

"Is that her?" asked Clyde.

"That is! That's her!" cheered Barkley. Each of the pups jumped and yapped with delight.

The words *Jasmine Johnson* shined beside the picture. Then her profile appeared.

 JASMINE JOHNSON
Age: 8
Grade: Third (but in 3rd/4th grade combo class)
School: Cloverfield Elementary
Problem: Best friend moved away

The Crystal Bone projected scenes of Jasmine Johnson and another girl onto the side of the classroom building. The two of them smiled and laughed, danced and sang. They wore aprons and baked cookies and cupcakes together. Another scene showed the pair rescuing a turtle from a busy street. They carefully placed the turtle in a pond and watched it swim away.

Rosie took her paws from the Crystal Bone and cupped them in front of her.

A glittering hologram showed Jasmine and the other girl hugging each other tightly. Then the other girl climbed into a truck. The two waved at each other as the truck, loaded with suitcases and furniture, drove away.

"Even though she is also in third grade, the Crystal Bone said that Jasmine is in Mrs. Anderson's third-and-fourth-grade combination class," said Rosie.

"That would explain why we didn't see her before," said Barkley.

"Her best friend moved away last week," continued Rosie, dropping down onto all fours and pacing back and forth between the Crystal Bone and the pups. "Hmm. Let's think about this, Pups. Meiko is in the third grade. Jasmine is in the third grade."

"Good fit there," said Noodles. "Meiko doesn't have anyone to play with since she's new. Jasmine doesn't have anyone to play with because her bestie moved away."

"True," said Rosie. "Also, Meiko and Jasmine both like to sing and dance."

"And they both like animals," added Clyde.

"All good points, Pups," said Rosie. Meiko and Jasmine did seem to have a lot in common.

"And the most important part of all," said Barkley, "they both need a friend!"

"Exactly!" said Rosie.

"But," began Clyde, his face scrunched up with more questions, "how DO you make a friend?"

"Give a nice gift?" suggested Noodles.

"That could work!" added Rosie. "What else could you do to make a friend?"

The pups thought harder. They were good at making friends. As a matter of fact, the four of them were Best Friends Furever. Plus, anytime a human spotted the pups, they wanted to keep the pups as pets. Friend-making was a piece of cake for them.

"Well, if you didn't know someone and you wanted to be their friend, you could go up to them and say hi," said Noodles.

"Yeah, and ask their name!" added Clyde. "Like this." He hurried over to Noodles and said, "Hi, Noodles, I'm Clyde. What's your name?"

"Noodles," answered the labradoodle. "Nice to meet you." All four pups chuckled with glee.

"That's good!" said Rosie. "What else?"

"You could see if they like the same things as you," said Barkley. "I like bones."

"ME TOO!" called all the pups at the same time, waggling their tails like crazy.

"See. I guess that's why *we* are all friends," said Rosie. They all 100 percent agreed that bones were the best!

"You could also ask someone if they want to play. Or share your toys with them," added Noodles.

All good ideas. But would Meiko do any of those things? How could they help her try these ideas out without getting caught?

One thing was very clear to the pups: Jasmine and Meiko were a perfect match! But since they were in separate classes, it wouldn't be easy to get the girls to meet.

"I bet all the third graders have recess and lunch at the same time," said Rosie. "They probably even have PE together, too. And best of all, look," she said pointing her paw at a large poster on the fence. "Tonight is their Spaghetti Dinner Bonanza."

"What's a Dinner Bone-anza?" asked Clyde.

"Bonanza," corrected Barkley, "and I have no idea."

Rosie didn't know either. "Bone, what *is* a Spaghetti Dinner Bonanza?" She placed her paws on the Bone and closed her eyes.

"Oh, I see," she said, pulling her paws from the crystal. "It's when everybody from school comes back at night with their families," said Rosie. "They all eat spaghetti and watch a movie together."

"Sounds yummy," said Clyde.

"And guess what? The Bonanza has a three-legged friend race!" Rosie cupped her glowing paws to show a hologram of kids hopping side by side, their legs tied together with a string. "All the kids pair up with a friend to compete against the adults for prizes."

The pups twittered as they watched the hologram pair falling over with laughter while trying to hop down the field.

"Well, if the three-legged race is tonight, that means we only have today to help the girls become friends so they can enter it together," said Noodles.

That didn't give the Love Puppies much time. They needed to come up with some ideas—and right away!

"How can we help Meiko and Jasmine meet?" asked Rosie.

"Maybe we can put a leash on them and walk them to the same spot?" answered Clyde.

"We can't leash human children," Rosie giggled. "That idea is a Saint Bernard–sized no."

"What if we act like sheepdogs and herd them?" asked Barkley.

"Also a no," answered Noodles. "They'd probably think they were being chased by a wild puppy parade."

"And we probably couldn't do that without being seen," added Barkley. Another good point.

"I've got it!" said Rosie, wagging her tail with

excitement. "I know how we can get the girls to meet!"

The pups gathered around Rosie, barely able to hide their enthusiasm.

"Both girls seem to like flowers, right?" That was clear at morning recess. "Well, that's perfect for my plan. We'll need two plants, two urgent notes, and an empty school garden. We can do it during lunchtime!"

Rosie explained the whole plan to the pups.

"Yes," she finished, "girls in the garden + at the same time = instant friendship."

Chapter 6
Planting a Plan

The plan was simple enough: help the girls meet up in the garden.

The pups jumped through the Doggie Door for supplies. Back at the Doghouse, the Love Puppies got right to work.

"Clyde, pots, please," said Rosie. "Noodles, dirt. And Barkley . . ."

But before she could finish, Barkley's paws began to glow. His long body morphed into a bright purple typewriter. Rosie barked with approval and grabbed two pieces of paper.

"All right, Barkley. This is what the note should say."

> Dear Jasmine,
>
> Please plant this in the school garden as soon as possible so we can show everybody at the Bonanza tonight. Thank you.
>
> Sincerely,
> Mrs. Anderson

Typewriter-Barkley's keys clicked away as magic ink wrote out the message. Next, he typed another letter with the same message. Except it was written to Meiko from "Mrs. Nicholson."

"Paw-fect!" said Rosie as she looked over the note.

"Here are the pots," called Clyde, flying into the Love Puppy den. He swooped around the room while balancing the pots on each of his upturned paws—almost bumping Noodles.

"Hey, careful," Noodles squealed through her teeth as she tugged a blanket that held a mound of dirt. Noodles carefully pulled the dirt along the floor toward Rosie and Barkley.

With orange-glowing paws, Noodles sent a breeze to lift the dirt into the pots. Next, Rosie wiggled her nose and up grew two perfect Pilea friendship plants, one in each pot.

Barkley changed himself into a wagon. "Load me up," he said.

With outstretched paws and the magic words, off went the Love Puppies—*whoosh!*

The pups landed outside the cafeteria with the plants in tow. They sneaked a glance inside. On one side of the room sat a lonesome-looking Meiko. And on the other sat Jasmine, all by herself, too.

"There!" whispered Rosie, pointing at a cafeteria cart.

Barkley morphed into a blanket that matched the cafeteria floor and covered Clyde, who'd grabbed the friendship plants. Without being seen, Clyde and Blanket-Barkley swooped into action. They carefully soared toward the cart, and then hid beside it. Rosie and Noodles positioned themselves out of sight and behind the door.

"On three," whispered Rosie. "One, two, three!"

Right at the exact same time, Rosie and Noodles let out the loudest, cutest puppy howl they could. "Oww, oww, wooooooooo!" they cried.

Meiko, Jasmine, and all the other humans looked toward the door.

"What's that?" someone called.

"Sounds like puppies," said another.

While everyone was distracted, Clyde and Barkley

had just enough time to put the plan into motion. Clyde zoomed over to Jasmine and placed one of the plants in the perfect spot next to her tray. Barkley raced to do the same for Meiko. Then, the clever pups hurried back outside without being seen.

"Where did this come from?" asked Meiko, touching the pot. She opened the note and read it. Instantly, she got up, packed her things, dumped her tray, and carried the plant outside.

"Meiko's on the move," whispered Rosie. "So far, so good."

Meanwhile, Jasmine read her note and placed it back onto the table. Then she took another bite of her sandwich.

"What is she doing?" whispered Noodles. "She's not getting up."

"Looks like she's finishing her lunch," said Barkley.

"She must be really hungry," whispered Clyde. His mouth watered at the thought of a bite of Jasmine's sandwich. "It looks like chicken. Mmmm, chicken."

"Poodle-sticks!" whimpered Barkley. "Jasmine is going to miss her chance."

"Don't worry, Pups," said Rosie. "We still have time."

At least Rosie hoped they did. Meiko was a fast walker and Rosie was sure she'd be planting the Pilea in the school garden any second now.

Rosie wished with all her heart that Jasmine would make it in time!

Once Jasmine's tray was empty, she stood up. She cleaned off her area and grabbed her things. Then she carefully picked up the plant and headed out the door. The pups followed closely behind, keeping to the shadows. It was clear Jasmine had no idea the four fuzzy-pup tails were tracking her every move.

When Jasmine reached the schoolyard, the pups chased after her through the grassy field, hidden again by a green Blanket-Barkley and Rosie-grown grass.

"There's the garden!" whispered Noodles. "And look, Meiko is still there!"

"Our plan is working," said Clyde with delight in his bark.

But just as Jasmine approached the front gate, Meiko walked toward the back exit. Uh-oh!

"I didn't know there was more than one way in and out," cried Noodles.

"I'm on it," called Rosie. She let out a giant yip, catching both Jasmine's and Meiko's attention. With both girls distracted, Rosie wiggled her nose like the Easter Bunny. The vines of a giant sweet pea plant began to grow and grow. Soon, it blocked the back exit completely.

Meiko turned and spotted the quickly growing plant. "Oh my!" She stumbled backward, backward, backward and crashed right into Jasmine.

"Oof!" cried Jasmine. The two-girl collision sent

the friendship plant flying, both it and Jasmine spilling onto the ground.

"Oh!" cried Meiko. "I didn't mean to. I am so sorry! I got frightened. I thought I saw—" Meiko's cheeks turned bright red. She covered her face and dashed from the garden, leaving Jasmine behind. Meiko didn't look back. Not even once.

"Well, that was rude," said Jasmine to one of the school's chickens as it came clucking by. She watched Meiko rush across the field and out of sight.

"Did you see that, Miss Fluffy-Fingers?" Jasmine said, folding her arms across her chest. "Didn't even offer to help or ask if I was okay." Still seated, Jasmine reached for the corn feed bag nearby and

dropped some kernels for Miss Fluffy-Fingers,
causing the chicken to come in closer.

"Mmmm, corn," whispered Clyde, eyeing the
kernels that Miss Fluffy-Fingers pecked on the
ground. Clyde's tummy rumbled loudly.

"Focus, Clyde," said Rosie. "We've got a problem
on our paws." If Jasmine thought Meiko was rude,
there was no way she'd want to be friends with her.
And Rosie was pretty sure knocking a plant out of
someone's hands was *not* the way to start a friendship.

"Who was that girl, anyway?" said Jasmine,
standing and dusting dirt from her pants. "Somebody
with no manners—that's for sure!" Jasmine shook her
head. She couldn't see Meiko anymore, but she could

see the other kids clearing out of the cafeteria and onto the playground. "Well, Miss Fluffy-Fingers, better get this cleaned up before lunch is over."

"That didn't go as planned," whispered Barkley.

Mission Meiko was proving to be a *whole* lot harder than the pups had thought it would be.

"What are we going to do now, Rosie?" asked Clyde.

Rosie's shoulders dropped as she looked away from her puppy team. She let out an extra-long sigh that she had been holding in. What *were* they going to do now?

Rosie was fresh out of ideas.

Chapter 7
Do-Si-Don't

Feeling low, the pups went back to their hideout behind the bushes outside Room 13. Lunch was over and their plan had been as bad as having to take a cold doggie bath.

"Too bad that didn't work," said Clyde. He lay on

his back looking up at the sky, watching hamburger-shaped clouds drifting by.

"Do you think a human kid could dry up like a thirsty flower if they cried all day, every day?" asked Rosie. She sadly petted the petals of a rose she had just grown.

"Maybe Meiko can make a friend next year," said Barkley.

"Or over the summer," said Clyde.

But then, the idea of Meiko spending time with her old friends floated into each pup's mind. Dancing and singing. Laughing and playing. Baking a cake and taking a giant bite, smiling a chocolate-covered smile.

When Rosie thought about Meiko remaining

friendless for the rest of the school year, a now-familiar twinge tickled her chest and her paws began to glow. The flickering pink hologram that appeared showed Meiko in the restroom, hugging her knees and crying. After a long moment, she stood, pushed a bathroom stall door open, and walked out with her head down.

"She must be feeling so sad right now," said Rosie as she watched the hologram.

The pups whimpered and whined. It broke their tender hearts to see the girl so blue.

"But we can't give up on her. She needs our help!" reminded Rosie.

Just then, children's voices caused the pups' ears

to stand up tall. They watched as rows of third and fourth graders walked onto the field in straight lines. Meiko stood at the end of Mrs. Nicholson's line, her eyes all red and her head still hanging low.

"Look! There's Jasmine, too!" said Barkley.

The pups watched as Mr. Barnett pushed a button on a giant speaker he had wheeled out. Twangy music started to play. Then Mr. Barnett began moving his feet.

"Must be time for PE," said Noodles.

"But what is he doing?" Clyde asked.

Barkley giggled. "I think he's . . . square-dancing."

Mr. Barnett called out to the children and each of them started copying the teacher's moves: step, step, kick. Step, step, kick. Twirl, twirl, twirl. Step, step, kick.

Soon, everyone was dancing and smiling—even Meiko! The children added in a new move, hooking arms and swinging around in a circle before switching to another partner.

"That's it!" called Noodles. "We'll get them to swing together. And I know exactly how! Come with me, Clyde."

Noodles hopped onto Clyde's back. Her paws glowed orange as a fog swirled around them. As soon as they were close enough, Noodles took a deep breath. Then, she blew a strong tornado wind that spun only Jasmine, turning her around and around.

As Jasmine twirled, she got closer and closer to Meiko.

"Come on," urged Noodles. "A little bit more . . . PAW-FECT!" With a clap, Noodles stopped the wind and calmed the air.

Even though the tornado had stopped, Jasmine kept spinning. She was so dizzy, she stumbled past Meiko . . . and fell right into a puddle of mud. *SPLASH!*

"Oopsie-poopsie!" said Noodles. "Too much spin."

Meiko looked on in horror as the wet and mushy mud oozed down Jasmine's back.

"Are you okay?" asked Meiko.

Jasmine didn't speak. She sat on the ground,

stone-still. Then, out of nowhere, she burst into laughter. The kind that wobbled a human's whole body and made their face hurt from smiling when someone told them the best joke ever. As Jasmine laughed, she shook glops of mud from her hands.

"That was quite a landing, Jazzy," said Mrs. Anderson as she and a few other classmates came over to help her up.

"I don't know what happened." Jasmine laughed again. "But that was *way* too much fun!"

"That spinning was amazing," said a boy with glasses.

"You could have been an ice-skater!" said his identical twin brother.

"Did you see that splash—mud went everywhere!" Jasmine grinned, wiping the stuff from her pants.

"Head to the nurse's office," said Mrs. Anderson. "She can get you all cleaned up."

Meiko watched as a muddy Jasmine walked with the twins toward the front office. This time Jasmine didn't look back. She hadn't answered Meiko's question either.

Rosie began to wonder if these two girls actually were a good match after all. And if not, who would be Meiko's friend?

Chapter 8
Cake-tastrophe

"I thought that was going to work for sure," said Noodles. She and Clyde had rejoined the rest of the pups. After Jasmine's epic fall, Mr. Barnett turned off the music, and the kids and their teachers headed inside.

"It was a really good try," said Rosie. But she could not hide the concern in her voice.

"What else could we do to bring the girls together?" asked Barkley. "We already tried plants. Howl-rrible fail. And dancing didn't work either!"

"We could do something with food," Clyde suggested.

"That's your answer to everything," Noodles giggled.

"It isn't my fault. A full belly just makes everything better," replied Clyde.

Since everybody else was out of ideas, the Love Puppies decided to take Clyde's suggestion.

"What were you thinking?" asked Rosie.

"We could bake a cake," Clyde offered.

"A cake?" replied Rosie. "Clydie, you're a genius! We already know both girls like to bake."

"And *eat* their creations—eat them all up!" Clyde repeated. "We could make a strawberry and vanilla cake sprinkled with bacon and dog bone bits!" His mouth watered at the thought.

"I'm not sure if human kids would like bacon and dog bones on a cake," said Rosie. "But strawberries and vanilla might do the trick! Let's do it! I'm willing to try anything. Homeward we go!"

Back at the Doghouse, the pups worked together to bake the cake.

"Eggs," called Rosie. Three of them floated and

81

bobbed through the air, dancing in a flying ballet on a gust of wind courtesy of Noodles.

"Check!" replied Noodles, wiggling her nose and causing the eggs to carefully crack into a bowl.

"Flour and sugar," Rosie called.

Two miniature, white tornados twirled out of the pantry, stopped above the counter, and dropped into the bowl.

"Check and check," said Noodles.

"Can I help?" asked Barkley, who'd transformed himself into a purple whisk.

"Let's do it!" said Noodles. She lifted Whisk-Barkley into the air and blew a gale that spun him around and around.

"Wooo-hooo!" laughed Barkley. This cake-flavored Tilt-A-Whirl was better than any amusement park ride he'd ever been on!

"Finally, a successful spin," cheered Noodles. She still felt bad about making Jasmine spin out of control and right into a muddy bath.

After all the ingredients had been combined, the Love Puppies baked their creation. Finally, Clyde frosted the cake carefully with vanilla icing. He even added little bone-shaped candies for decoration. "This looks almost too good to eat!" he panted. *Almost!* he repeated, licking his chops.

Once it was finished, the pups gathered around and woofed with glee.

"It's beautiful!" said Noodles, her tongue hanging out with excited approval.

"You sure about leaving off the bacon bits?" asked Clyde.

"Certain," replied Rosie.

"Now we're ready to give Meiko a very sweet surprise," said Barkley, bringing over a box and another typed note that said: "To Meiko, From Jasmine." Once the cake was safe in the box, Rosie opened the Doggie Door, and the pups headed back to the school.

This plan just *had* to work!

Back outside Cloverfield Elementary, the Love Puppies found the third and fourth graders in the cafeteria again. Some were eating their snack. Others helped the teachers hang up decorations for the Bonanza. Jasmine leaned against the far wall, taping up streamers and giant paper flowers. She had changed out of the muddy clothes into clean ones.

Meiko sat on the other end of the room, eating crackers . . . and not talking to anyone.

"There they are," said Rosie. "Ready, Noodles?"

The labradoodle took a big breath and blew the cake up high, so it hovered near the ceiling, unnoticed. Slowly and carefully, she floated it closer and closer to Meiko.

"Almost there," said Barkley.

The cake inched nearer and nearer.

"You are bad to the bone—but in a good way!" celebrated Clyde, jumping with excitement. "You can do it!"

As he landed on the ground, a cloud of dust rose and reached Noodles's nose.

"A-a-ACHOO!" went Noodles.

And *CRASH* went the cake. It toppled out of the box and onto a kid sitting down eating his yogurt.

"Hey! What the . . ." the boy said, twirling around to see where the cake had come from. "What did you do that for, Jaime?" he asked another boy standing nearby.

"Wasn't me, Carlos—" Jaime started to say. But it

was too late. Carlos hurled his yogurt, splashing the other boy in a creamy mess.

"FOOD FIGHT!" yelled a voice. And right before the Love Puppies' eyes, total chaos erupted across the cafeteria. Milk cartons sloshed through the air. Apple slices bounced off foreheads. Hummus oozed down the walls.

Meiko, Jasmine, and a few other kids dodged the flying food and ran for the door.

"Uh-oh!" said Rosie. "This isn't good."

Another failed plan. And a really messy one at that. Rosie and the pups hurried outside to avoid getting hit, too.

Absolutely nothing was going as planned and

time was running out! The pups had tried three different ideas for Mission Meiko, and each plan had been a bigger failure than the one before it.

"We're gonna need to think of something new!" said Rosie, looking at the faces of her puppy crew as they hid behind a tree. "Wait! Where's Clyde?"

"I'm here! I'm here," he called, flying toward them. He was covered in sticky applesauce, crackers, yogurt, and juice. And his tummy bulged big and full. "Sorry. I couldn't resist."

The others couldn't resist either. They hurried over to him, licking the tasty food off his fur.

"That tickles," Clyde giggled.

Once he was all tidied up, the pups refocused.

"I'm just not sure why our plans aren't working," said Noodles.

"Yeah," added Clyde. "We tried a gift—"

"TWO gifts if you count the friendship plant and the cake," interjected Barkley. "But no luck there."

"Spin dancing and garden meeting didn't go very well either," added Clyde.

"And Meiko still hasn't even said hi or told Jasmine her name," said Noodles.

"Maybe we are going about this all wrong," said Rosie. "Maybe nothing will work if there's somebody planning things behind the scenes."

"Oh, you mean because you can't force people to be friends?" said Noodles.

Rosie smiled. "Righto, Noodles. Friendships are best when you make them by yourself."

"Is there a way we can get the girls to meet and then let them take it from there?" Barkley asked.

But before the pups could answer, a loud scream tore through the air. They knew right away who it was. With all the time they had spent learning about her, they could certainly recognize her voice.

"Meiko's in trouble!" cried Rosie.

Chapter 9
Not-So-Fast Friends

The pups dashed in the direction of the scream: the cafeteria. Was Meiko all right? It sounded like something really bad had happened.

Staying out of sight, the pups huddled by the window to look inside.

They could see Meiko sitting on the ground in a pile of cake, looking dazed.

Jasmine hurried over. "Are you okay?" she asked.

"Yes, I think so," answered Meiko. "I slipped on this mess when I was trying to clean it up. Where did this cake come from, anyway?"

Jasmine reached for a note next to the empty box.

"That's so strange," she said. "It says 'To Meiko, From Jasmine.'"

Meiko's eyes widened at Jasmine's words.

"Wait—I'm Meiko. You're telling me that this cake was for me?"

"I guess so. But *I'm* Jasmine, and I didn't send you a cake. I didn't even know it was your birthday!"

"Oh," said Meiko, looking a little disappointed.

"Maybe Jasmine Ortega sent it."

"Maybe," said Meiko. "And actually, it isn't my birthday. My birthday is January 30th—but I do really like cake."

Jasmine gasped and looked at Meiko. "*My* birthday is January 30th," she said, "and I really like cake, too!"

"Really?" said Meiko.

"Really," said Jasmine. "Hi, I'm Jasmine Johnson."

"Hi. I'm Meiko Ito. It's nice to meet you." She smiled.

"You too," said Jasmine. "You look kind of familiar."

Meiko could have sworn she'd met Jasmine before, too. But where? "Want to help me clean up this cake mess?" she finally asked.

"Sure," said Jasmine. "But first, do you want me to walk you to the nurse's office? You've got cake all over your pants. Nurse Rian will have an extra change of clothes."

"Okay," said Meiko.

With that, Jasmine walked toward her teacher and Meiko walked toward hers.

Outside the window, the pups jumped and bumped one another, trying to get a better view of what was happening.

"Why are they going separate ways?" asked Clyde,

who hovered above the ground and peered through the window.

"I bet they're just getting permission to go see the nurse," said Barkley.

"I hope so," said Rosie. "I'm really starting to think that we won't ever find a friend for Meiko."

Just then, the pups heard Meiko's familiar voice. "Come on, Pups!" called Rosie. She and her friends hurried to the hallway and hid as Meiko and Jasmine walked down the corridor.

Could it be? wondered Rosie. *Were they talking together? Were they . . . FRIENDS?*

"Today has been such a weird day," said Meiko. "I got a really strange plant with even stranger directions to bring it to the garden."

"Yeah, me too," said Jasmine. "Wait, were you the person who knocked me over and ran away?"

Meiko stopped in her tracks and went silent.

"That really hurt," said Jasmine.

Uh-oh, thought Rosie, *so much for fast friends.*

"I'm so sorry," said Meiko. "This other plant was growing super fast right in front of me. It was really odd, and I got kind of scared. I had to get out of there!"

"That's so . . . wild!" said Jasmine.

"Something like that happened earlier, too, when my class was at the garden," added Meiko.

Rosie could feel her puppy cheeks flush pink.

"I know how you feel," said Jasmine. "During gym class, a huge gust of wind kept spinning me around and around until I fell down. That has never happened to me before."

"I saw that! That was YOU?" said Meiko. "It was so cool that you just laughed it off. I would have cried for sure," she said.

"And we still don't know where that cake came from," said Jasmine, changing the subject.

"I don't know, but I wish it hadn't gone splat. That frosting was delicious!" Then, in a very small voice, Meiko added, "Do you, maybe, want to be my friend?"

Jasmine smiled. "With both of us having to go to

the nurse's office for new pants," she said, touching her fingers like she was counting, "and all the weird stuff happening to us today, I think we're meant to be friends, Meiko."

The Love Puppies' ears perked up.

"Did you hear that?!" said Rosie. "Our plans worked after all!"

"WE DID IT!" yelped Clyde before launching into a midair somersault. "Yip yip HOORAY!"

The loud bark echoed down the hallway, bouncing off the walls. Both girls spun around so quickly, the pups didn't have a chance to hide.

"Look!" cried Jasmine. "PUPPIES!"

Oh no! The Love Puppies' cover was blown!

Chapter 10
Furever Friendship

Jasmine and Meiko dashed toward the puppies.

"Look how cute they are!" said Meiko. She giggled

as she reached for one of the adorable pups.

Just then, Noodles blanketed the pups in a cloud

of fog to hide them from the girls. Then she kicked

up a breeze to gently blow the girls backward.

"How did that happen?" said Meiko. But the wild weather didn't stop her. Instead, she leaned into the wind and reached through the fog until her hands touched something soft, cuddly, and oh-so wiggly. It yelped as she pulled it from the cloud.

"Look at this chubby guy!" she said, showing Jasmine the squirmy shar-pei. Clyde wriggled and wiggled in her arms until Meiko could no longer hold him. "Oh no!" she said as he fell from her hands.

Instead of landing hard on the cement, the heart-shaped pads on Clyde's paws began to glow, and he swooped into the air just in time and flew back into the fog cloud.

"Did you see that?" asked Meiko, her eyes as wide as Frisbees.

Jasmine nodded with a confused look on her face. She had never seen a flying puppy before.

"Could this day get any stranger?" said Jasmine. "Giant growing plants, wind out of nowhere, flying cakes, *and* flying puppies? Whose paws can glow . . ."

Suddenly the confusion melted into a look of understanding. Jasmine giggled, and in a confident voice, she said, "It's too late. We've seen you. No need to hide."

When the puppies didn't move, Jasmine tried again. "We are on to you, cute puppies. You are magic! You *have* to be! Nothing else could explain this weirdo day. So come on out. We're very friendly. We won't hurt you."

With that, the breeze died down and the fog cloud expanded to wrap around the girls, too. No one could see Jasmine and Meiko or the four pups who looked up at them with giant puppy dog eyes.

Rosie stepped forward and sat down right in front of the girls. She could feel her puppy heart pound in her chest, but it wasn't from being scared. It felt more like love and kindness spreading from these two girls to her. The tingle she'd felt in her chest that morning returned and warmed her all over.

She looked back at her puppy crew, and the look on their puppy faces told her they felt it, too. Something about these girls made them feel stronger and more magical than ever.

"Rosie, look!" barked Barkley, raising a paw and motioning to her chest.

Rosie looked down. An outline of a vibrant pink heart glowed brightly across her fur. With each step Jasmine and Meiko took toward her, the heart grew brighter, until slowly and gently, both girls wrapped their arms around Rosie and her whole body began to glow.

The other puppies gasped. They had known Rosie all her life, but they had never seen anything like this.

It was as if the love and kindness in each of the

girls' hearts connected with Rosie like she had never experienced before. Rosie wondered if this was what being truly loved by a human really felt like. Could Meiko and Jasmine feel it, too?

Rosie lifted her paws, one toward each girl. And soon they were holding hands.

"We are the Love Puppies," said Rosie. "And I think we were meant to be friends—*all* of us. You, me, Barkley, Noodles, and Clyde." Each pup waved a paw as Rosie made introductions.

By now, the other pups had joined the circle. They, too, glowed with the shine of new friendship.

"You weren't supposed to see us," said Rosie, "but now that you have, you must keep us a secret."

"Are you superhero puppies?" asked Jasmine.

"No," said Rosie, "not superheroes. But we do help children by spreading love, kindness, and friendship wherever we go. Today, our mission was to help Meiko find a friend."

Meiko's cheeks blushed at Rosie's words.

"Mission accomplished," replied Jasmine, smiling at Meiko.

"Whenever children are in need, we use our magic to help when we can," continued Rosie.

"That sounds pretty super to me," said Jasmine.

"What I didn't know," continued Rosie, "is that we needed you, too." The warm glow traveled around the circle from hand to paw. It swirled inside Rosie's heart—a feeling that was new and powerful! Maybe helping kids in need wasn't just a mission. Maybe it *was* their true superpower. But, it was clear today that it was love that made the puppies' magic work. For the first time ever, Rosie truly understood how lucky she and her friends were.

But to keep the magic alive, they'd need Meiko's and Jasmine's help.

"If you tell anyone about us, our magic will go away forever." Each of the puppies whimpered at Rosie's words.

"I promise not to tell," said Jasmine.

"Me too," said Meiko. "Cross my heart."

Suddenly, heart pendants glowed around each of

the pups' necks like necklaces made of light. Then, two actual necklaces appeared around Rosie's neck.

"For you," she told Meiko and Jasmine.

The girls gently pulled the necklaces from Rosie's soft fur. One side of the heart-shaped charm said:

$$LP + MI + JJ = BFFs$$

The other side had four paw prints, each one in the signature color of one of the Love Puppies, and two human handprints.

Meiko held the necklace to her heart and closed her eyes. She hadn't gained just one friend today—she'd gotten five. "I will keep your secret for always."

"Thank you," yelped Clyde. "And who knows, we

just might turn up to check on you again someday."
All the pups knew this to be true, even though in
the past, they never returned to a human child after
a mission was completed.

Rosie smiled. "No matter what, we'll never be far
from your hearts."

With that, all the puppies charged the girls and
covered them in soft, puppy kisses. The girls hugged
and kissed them back.

This was definitely a friendship that would last
forever—Rosie was sure of it.

Chapter 11
Mission Accomplished

Back at the Doghouse, the pups sat quietly, nibbling on their dinner. Each of them was still thinking about Meiko and Jasmine, and the beautiful moment they had shared.

A quick peek at the Crystal Bone had shown

that the Bonanza had been a tail-wagging success. Jasmine and Meiko introduced each other to their families and then stayed by each other's side the whole night—just like BFFs would. Then, they took first place in the three-legged race and won a pizza party for each of their classrooms!

"Pizza parties will definitely help them make even *more* friends," said Clyde. "I, for one, would be friends with anybody who gave me pizza."

"Of course you would, you silly pup!" said Noodles. "And yes—there's always room for more friends!"

The pups sat quietly for a moment, thinking about what that meant.

"Well, I didn't know we needed human friends," said Barkley, breaking the silence.

"Me neither," agreed Rosie. "But I sure am glad we found them." She knew she and her puppy crew would watch over those special girls from here on out.

"This mission proved to me that making new friends is not an easy thing to do," said Barkley. "But trying things, like saying hi, can really help!"

"Yeah!" added Clyde. "And introducing yourself."

"Sharing something you care about—like toys, gifts, even necklaces—is a great way to reach out," giggled Noodles. "And seeing if you have things in common."

"Or being really nice to each other. And saying sorry when you do something wrong. Even if it's hard," Barkley said.

Rosie stayed quiet for a minute more as the others chatted about what it means to be a friend and how to make one. She lay on the ground next to her bowl, her jaw resting on her paws. Then she said, "I think all that is true. But I also think to be a good friend, you have to open up your heart, even if it feels a little scary."

All the pups agreed.

It was getting late. The Love Puppies washed up and got ready for bed, and soon everyone was fast asleep. Everyone, except Rosie.

As she lay in her doggie bed, she inhaled deeply and smiled. She couldn't wait to see the girls again. Of course, tomorrow would be another day. Rosie was excited to help someone new. She had learned so much from this mission. And she had gained so much. Her heart was full!

As she dozed off into puppy-dreams, she touched her paw to her chest. The glowing heart on her fur lit up, and within it, Jasmine and Meiko appeared. They were each at their own homes, lying in their own beds, facing the ceiling with smiles on their faces.

Each girl gently touched the new piece of jewelry around her neck. The one that rested on her heart. As their fingers ran over the letters inscribed on the necklaces, Rosie's own heart warmed all over again.

The Love Puppies hadn't just helped Meiko and Jasmine find each other—the girls had helped the puppies understand what a new and true friendship was really all about.

And when friends could help each other like that? Well, that was a real superpower! One that was truly magical!

Want more Love Puppy magic?

Read on for a sneak peek at the next adventure!

Chapter 1
Relaxing to the Max

"Another mission in the doggie bag," said Noodles the labradoodle as she and the Love Puppy team hurried behind a large rosebush that grew in the corner of Leticia Smith's lawn.

"Yes!" said Rosie the golden retriever. "Job well

done, Pups!" Rosie swished her tail and each rosebud on the bush began to bloom. That was Rosie's specialty. She had magical flower power, which meant she could grow plants whenever and wherever she pleased.

As the leader of the Love Puppy team, Rosie looked warmly over each member of her squad. Clyde, the Shar-Pei, caught her eye as he took a celebratory flying flip and yipped, "we did it!" His magic gave him the ability to fly.

Rosie turned her gaze to Barkley, a miniature dachshund, who morphed into a purple pom-pom. Barkley's magic allowed him to transform into anything. Next, Rosie turned to Noodles who then blew a gentle breeze to ruffle Barkley's shiny frill. Noodles had the ability to control elements of the weather.

This Love Puppy team spent their days helping kids in need and they enjoyed every moment of it. But their favorite part was always right after they successfully completed a mission. It meant another human child was helped out of a tough situation— just as Leticia had been!

So right then and there, each pup's jaws hung open in glee.

"That had to be a record," said Noodles, her big, brown eyes shining. "We helped Leticia in the flick of a puppy's tail." She wiggled her tail with delight.

"I think we earned a nice vacation."

"A *pup*-cation!" added Barkley. "Complete with umbrellas," he said, morphing his body into an umbrella and then into a lounge chair, "relaxation—"

"—and lots of snacks!" chimed in Clyde. He swooped in to rest on Lounge Chair-Barkley. Barkley changed back into his puppy body, and the two wrestled on the ground playfully.

"Let's head back and do it!" said Rosie. She held her paw out in front. Her paw pads began to glow pink. "Come on, Pups!"

All of the pups held out their paws, too, in the center of their puppy huddle. Each of their pads glowed like Rosie's: Noodles's orange, Clyde's blue, and Barkley's purple. "With the power of love—anything is possible. Love Puppies, go!"

As the magical portal known as the Doggie Door opened and the pups jumped through, off in the distance an anxious voice shouted: "Maxie! Maxie, come back!"

But the Love Puppies didn't hear the cry. Instead, with a *whoosh* and a flash of light and fur, the puppies transported from the human world back to the Doghouse—Love Puppy Headquarters—and landed in their backyard. Their pup-cation started now!

Rosie padded across the yard toward her vegetable garden beside the house. The first-floor living room window overlooked her bountiful display of plants. Noodles's room had a garden view, too, but on the second floor.

"Hello, my beauties," Rosie said as her magic caused the plants to dance and wave to her. She was eager to give them some extra tender love and care.

She used her teeth to grab her straw hat that hung on the wall and tossed it in the air. It fell right onto her head, her ears poking up through the Rosie-sized ear holes. She stopped next to her blossoming tomato plant and inhaled deeply. "How about a nice drink?" she asked as she reached for the hose.

Meanwhile, Clyde flew through the air toward two large trees with a hammock strung between them. Balanced on his upturned paws, he held a tray of goodies he had grabbed from the kitchen. With a flying flip—and not one treat out of place—he landed on the hammock, tummy up. He placed the tray on his belly and called out: "Noodles—glasses me!"

Noodles, who was tanning beside the bone-shaped pool, giggled and blew a huge gust of wind Clyde's way. This caused the sunglasses that were resting on the poolside table to take flight, tumble through the air, and land right on Clyde's eyes. Now the hammock rocked gently from the wind.